To Grandmama - thank you for all the books
(and for the wonderful paper they were always wrapped in!) - M A

For Joe & Flynn, watch out for those giants! - M C

LITTLE TIGER PRESS • 1 The Coda Centre, 189 Munster Road, London SW6 6AW
www.littletiger.co.uk • First published in Great Britain 2014
This edition published in the United States 2014

Text by Mara Alperin • Text copyright © Little Tiger Press 2014

Illustrations copyright © Mark Chambers 2014

Mark Chambers has asserted his right to be identified as the illustrator of this work
under the Copyright, Designs and Patents Act, 1988 • All rights reserved

ISBN 978-1-4351-5723-1 • Printed in Shenzhen, China • LTP/1900/1029/0814

Lot # 2 4 6 8 10 9 7 5 3 1
07/14

Jack and the Beanstalk

Adapted by Mara Alperin

Illustrated by Mark Chambers

LITTLE TIGER PRESS
London

Deep in the countryside lived
a widow and her son, Jack.
Their cottage was crumbling,
and their clothes were patched.
They were very, very poor.

One day, Jack's mother said, "We must
sell our cow. Take her to market, Jack,
and bring home some gold pieces."
And so he set off to town.

But before Jack had gotten very far, he met
a strange little man.

"That's a fine cow," the man said.
"I'll swap you five **magic beans** for her."

"Magic beans?" said Jack. "Are they
really magic?"

"Magic they are, or chop off my beard and knit it into a sweater," croaked the little man.

Magic beans!

Jack couldn't wait to tell his mother. He clutched them tightly, and ran all the way home.

Jack's mother was **furious**.
"We need money, not useless old beans!"
she cried. And she threw them out
of the window in disgust.

But late that night, a tiny bean sprout poked out from the ground.

and GREW!

and grew...

And then it grew...

The next morning, the beanstalk stretched high into the sky.

"The beans *were* magic!" Jack cried. "But what's at the top?"

Jack climbed up, up, up the

beanstalk.

At last, he reached the very top.
There, shimmering in the
sunlight, was . . .

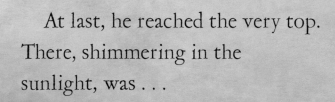

...a magnificent castle!

Just then, Jack's stomach rumbled.
I must find some breakfast, he thought,
and he tapped on the castle door.

The door creaked open, and a huge giantess smiled down.

"Hello!" Jack shouted up. "Please, do you have any food?"

"YOU POOR THING!" boomed the giantess. "COME RIGHT IN! BUT QUICKLY, BEFORE THE GIANT GETS UP!"

What a marvelous feast! There was an **enormous** loaf of bread and a **gigantic** jar of jelly. Jack dug in at once.

But suddenly, the room began to shake.

BOom!
BOom!
BOom!

"OH MY GOODNESS!" cried the giantess. "HE'S COMING!"

And she shoved Jack under a teacup to hide.

Into the room stomped a
big, scary, HUNGRY giant!

"FEE FI FO FUM!

I smell the blood of an Englishman!" he said.
"Be he alive, or be he dead,
I'll grind his bones to
make my bread!"

   "Don't be silly – there's nobody
here but us," the giantess scolded.
"Now go and wash before
breakfast!"

Jack trembled. *I must leave—now!* he thought. He was halfway down the hall when he heard a . . .

"SQUAWK!"

It was a hen with bright golden feathers!

"Help!" she clucked. "Set me free and I'll lay you golden eggs every morning!"

Jack scooped up the hen, but then he heard huge footsteps **THUNDERING** after them . . . .

"FEE FI FO FUM!"

roared the giant.

"I smell the blood of an Englishman...

AND THERE HE IS!"

Jack raced out of the door. He jumped . . .

...and slid
down the
beanstalk...

down...

down...

...all
the
way
back
to his

cottage.

down...

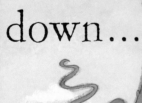

"Mother!
Quick! Bring the ax!"
he shouted.

Jack's mother swung the ax at the beanstalk. **THWACK!** It shuddered and shook, and then the giant came tumbling down!

"FEEEEEEE

FI FO..." CRASH!

And that was the end of the giant.

Jack hugged his mother tight. "Look what I found!" he said, and he showed her the golden hen.

"Oh, Jack," said his mother. "I'm so glad you're safe. And you were right about those magic beans!"

So Jack, his mother, and the golden hen
all lived happily ever after. And with
lots of **golden eggs**, they were
never poor again!

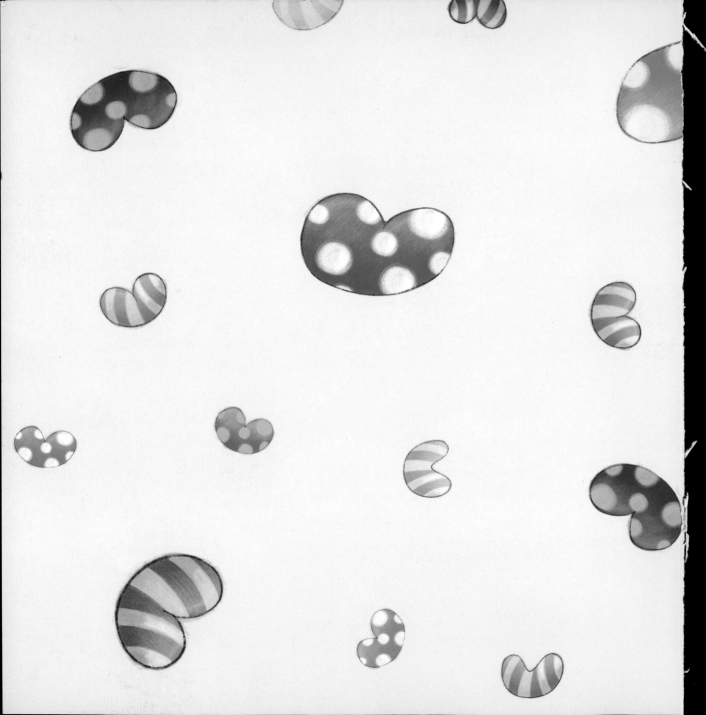